This book belongs to:

Poppy Jackson

Written by Tim Bugbird.
Illustrated by Clare Fennell.
Designed by Annie Simpson.

Copyright © 2011

make believe ideas ltd

The Wilderness, Berkhamsted, Herts, HP4 2AZ, UK.

www.makebelieveideas.com

OoLa, the OWL who lost her Hoot!

Tim Bugbird · Clare Fennell

make
believe
ideas

Oola was tired after playing all night.

"Hoot! Hoot! It's bedtime!" she cried,

as she flew through

the trees back to her nest.

It was nearly dawn

and the forest was waking up,

but Oola could only think

about her cosy bed.

Safely home, Oola smiled

as Mummy Owl gently tucked her

under a mossy blanket.

"Sleep tight, Little One,"

said Mummy Owl.

"Love you, Mum," said Oola,

in a tired little voice.

"H...h...h...."

Oola frowned.

Try as she might, she could not hoot.

"Don't worry," said Mummy Owl.

"You've been **flying** and **calling**

so much, you've

lost your hoot.

Now, **get some rest!**

You've tired

yourself out."

Oola was too worried to sleep.

"How can I have lost my hoot?" she wondered.
"I know — it must have been while I was playing.
I'll fly back and find it."

Oola waited until Mummy Owl wasn't looking,

then flew silently into the forest.

"Wow! This is amazing!"

thought Oola.

She had never

flown in daylight before

and everything looked

bright and **exciting**.

The **sun** filled the sky with
smudges of yellow and gold, and the trees
were a hundred shades of green.
Below her, **beautiful flowers** covered the
ground like a patchwork quilt.

As Oola swooped down to take a closer look…

she saw a tiny brown mouse.

"I've lost my hoot,"
whispered Oola.

"Have you found it?"

"SQUEAK!

SQUEAK!

SQUEAK!"
            said the mouse.

Oola took a deep breath:

"H...h...hweak! Hweak!"

"No, that's not my hoot," she thought.

The mouse giggled and scampered into the bushes.

Oola flew on towards the pond. Maybe her hoot was there.

At the water's edge, Oola saw a speckled frog,

sitting on a giant lily pad.

"I've lost my hoot," whispered Oola. "Have you found it?"

The frog looked at Oola,
puffed himself up,
and croaked,

"RIBBIT!

RIBBIT!

RIBBIT!"

Oola was
so startled,
she nearly jumped
out of her feathers!

"Oh, my!" thought Oola.

She opened her beak as wide as she could.

"H…h…hibbit! Hibbit!" she croaked.

"No, that's not my hoot," said Oola,

her voice so quiet that the frog could barely hear her.

Oola carried on through the forest
until she saw a **bendy-legged** grasshopper,
jumping in the grass.

"I've lost my hoot,"
whispered Oola.

"Have you found it?"

The grasshopper looked at Oola and **bounced** so high,

he nearly poked her in the eye!

"CHIRRUP! CHIRRUP! CHIRRUP!" he said.

Oola was determined not to give up.

She opened her beak and... "H...h...hirrup! Hirrup!"

"No, that's not my hoot either," she thought.

Oola was very tired, but she had to **find her hoot**.

The **mouse** didn't have it, the **frog** didn't have it

and the **grasshopper** certainly didn't have it.

"I know – I'll look by the stream,"

thought Oola.

When she reached the **stream,** Oola saw a yellow **duck,**

having a wash in the water.

The duck said hello with a loud

QUACK! QUACK! QUACK!

Poor Oola didn't need to ask.

"That's definitely
not my hoot,"
she sighed.

At that moment,

Oola heard a gentle **hooting** sound.

"That's mine!" she thought.

"But where is it?"

The duck **quacked** again,

only this time even **louder**,

and waved his wings towards the **tallest** tree in the forest.

Oola set off.

As she flew, the hoot grew

louder and louder.

Sitting alone at the very top

of the tallest tree, she found a

big brown owl.

"HOOT! HOOT!"
said the owl.

It was the loudest,

hootiest hoot

Oola had ever heard!

"This must be mine!"

thought Oola.

She opened her beak:

"H...h...h...."

Nothing!

Oola started to cry.

The big brown owl thought for a moment.

"Have you **lost your hoot**, Little Owl?" he asked.

Oola nodded.

"Well, don't cry, you can **share mine**.

Try hooting with me!"

The big brown owl coughed, took a deep breath
and **hooted** at the top of his voice.

Oola coughed, took a deep breath and…still **nothing**.

"**Try again!**" said the big brown owl.

So Oola coughed, took a big, deep breath and…

"HOOT! HOOT! HOOT!" she gasped.

"I've found it! Thank you! Thank you,
Brown Owl."

Oola couldn't wait to

get back to the nest

and tell Mummy Owl

she had found her hoot!

She flew through the forest, hooting as she swept past the trees, the stream and the 'pond.

until finally she was home.

Mummy Owl was waiting
inside the nest.

"Where have you been, Oola?"
she asked.
"I've been so worried about you!"

"I went searching for my hoot, and I found it!"
said Oola, proudly.

Mummy Owl laughed and gave Oola a big owl hug.
"Thank goodness you're home," she said.
"I've been calling you all day
and I've nearly
lost my hoot!"

"Don't worry, Mum,"
said Oola with a loud HOOT! HOOT!
"You can always share mine!"

The end